Is God on The Way??

In A World Going Mad!

Lynda Like

Heavens Gate Press

Is God's Army on The Way??
In A World Going Mad!
All Rights Reserved.
Copyright © 2023 Lynda Like
v2.0

This is a work of fiction. Names, characters, businesses, places, events, locales, and incidents are either the products of the author's imagination or used in a fictitious manner. Any resemblance to actual persons, living or dead, or actual events is purely coincidental.

The opinions expressed in this manuscript are solely the opinions of the author and do not represent the opinions or thoughts of the publisher. The author has represented and warranted full ownership and/or legal right to publish all the materials in this book.

This book may not be reproduced, transmitted, or stored in whole or in part by any means, including graphic, electronic, or mechanical without the express written consent of the publisher except in the case of brief quotations embodied in critical articles and reviews.

Heavens Gate Press

ISBN: 978-0-578-27505-5

Cover Photo © 2023 www.gettyimages.com. All rights reserved - used with permission.

PRINTED IN THE UNITED STATES OF AMERICA

Part I

THE STORIES

The sun was shining brightly and there was a fresh morning breeze in the air as Freddy and Andy made their way to the park; with their parents and siblings in tow. They lived and grew up in the same small development near the high school. It was a cul-de-sac lined with ten houses constructed of ranchers and two story homes with newly mowed lawns, tall shade trees, flowers and basketball hoops hanging from each garage in the driveways. They would get together at the playground in the park nearby their house and they would play baseball or catch and sometimes football. All the normal games boys would play with themselves. There would be quarrels at times between the groups of boys playing sports. Each boy would be yelling over the other's voice as they glared at one another. Was there ever a sport between children without any quarrels or disruptions? There were always the families who would be nearby sitting at a picnic table smiling or laughing as they enjoyed a snack, bought from their homes, while their boys played together. Sometimes all the boy's parents couldn't make it but if they couldn't make it that day; it seemed a non verbal agreement was formed to take someone's child to the park that day. When the quarrels erupted as they inevitably would, the fathers would stand up from the table ready to go see what was going on but it was the mothers who held them back, letting the children work out their differences. There was a lot of yelling and sometimes they thought the kids would never find a solution. Letting them work out their problems took time but they saw that the kids did work out whose turn at bat it was or who was going to catch the ball the next time. Their parents were always there sitting at a table together. Other parents were sitting at tables around the park. They looked at this time as more of a social nature, getting to know their children's friends' parents, but also keeping an eye on their children. The kids could see their parents drinking coffee and smiling at each other. It was the usual routine they did throughout the warm months of summer. The boys both have younger sisters who would also play together on the sliding board or what the adults would call 'the jungle gym.' The parents were talking together about school starting soon and how it would give them a little break and things around the house could finally get done. This was the classic picture of America. The summer months turned into the beginning of fall and the start of school. Both boys would be entering second grade.

This year the 'meet the teacher' day was different. The greeting was very short and no talk of the curriculum for the kids. The room was very plain from what they were used to seeing. The teacher gave you five minutes and you were done. You were no longer allowed to browse the library to look at the books. We thought it was strange but we weren't concerned. Why would we be? School started and things seemed to be fine, until it wasn't. The second week found our boy complaining about his stomach hurting and he didn't want to go to school. We kept him home for that day. The teacher called to inquire why our son wasn't in school. We thought it odd but told her he was ill. The next day I found him crying about going to school. We sat down with him and had a talk. We said we thought you liked school Andy, what has happened to change your mind. It didn't come easily as Andy put his finger up to his lips and then whispered very low he wasn't allowed to talk about school. We finally heard what he had to say. It seems Andy was not to talk to Freddy anymore and they couldn't be friends because he has white skin. They were not to sit together at lunch anymore because he could hurt Andy. He said other boys had to sit in different seats too. Wait, What!! The parents called Freddy's parents and asked if they noticed anything different about Freddy. The only thing we noticed about Freddy was he's more quiet and seemed to be unhappy, his parents responded. They were concerned about Freddy. Andy's parents told them about their son and what was said to him by the teacher. They couldn't believe their ears. Freddy's parents turned to look at their son as they hung up the phone. Very careful as they asked Freddy if something was going on at the school that may have made him a little sad. Freddy said he couldn't talk about it or he would get in trouble with the teacher. Finally, after reassuring Freddy numerous times that nothing bad was going to happen to him because they were there to protect him from harm. All the while holding their anger inside so as not to upset Freddy even more; Freddy put his finger up to his lips and said, "Shush, don't tell anyone," she said, and then called me a white supremist and I have no rights and I am not to sit near a person of color. If I couldn't find a seat, I should take my chair into the corner and sit and stare at the wall. He began to cry. So infuriated were they that the mother called Andy's parents back and talked about what to do. They all decided to take their children down to the school themselves and talk to the teacher and the principal about this. When they entered the lobby they were told they could not enter any further. It was for the 'Safety of children.' "I'm sorry," Beth the secretary said, ``but the principal has given orders that no parents are allowed into the school." The children were let in and the parents could pick them up after school. Beth looked back at the two sets of parents and stated quietly she knows what is going on and she doesn't like it and will be handing in her resignation at the end of today. They then looked at one another and wondered what to do.

It wasn't long before children who walked with parents to school or dropped them off were talking and hearing about what they were teaching in schools to their children. These parents told the other parents dropping off their children that they weren't allowed in the school building at all. People started lining up and demanding to talk with the principal of the school. He refused to come out and called the police. The police came and told the parents they were trespassing on government property and causing a riot and under the law could be charged with domestic terrorism if they did not disperse. The people tried to tell the police what was going on but to no avail. They wouldn't allow the children to be taken back out of the school. So parents banned together that day and after a very noisy meeting said, "let's sue them." When the children were dropped off from school they didn't return the next day or the next. The school threatened them and said they could take their children away from them. The attorney's for the parents slapped an injunction on the school banning teachers from teaching children anything other than education based studies until they went to court. Hate based and divisive teaching would not be tolerated.

Bill and Karen were the parents of a son and daughter in a small community outside of a big city near them. Since a lot of things changed in their and others lives they were more careful about going to different places. They had friends in the neighborhood whom they would get together with for bar-be-ques or small picnics. Since the government changed hands in the last election, things were no longer normal. Crime was rampant in the larger cities and the legal system just wasn't interested in arresting anyone for crimes committed by angry protestors or gang related groups. They couldn't understand how their country had been broken down so quickly by this government. In church, the pastor talked about what was happening to our country and everyone had to stand firm against any wrongs they would encounter. He believed we were in the 'End of Days' portion of the bible. We all felt he was right, we believed we were living in the end of days too. We were not to engage in physical violence but to contact our representatives in office who still cared about the rule of law and to pray about our country. The church gave people a feeling of sanity in the midst of lawlessness and fear.

One day the FBI showed up at the church and said this church is shut down until further notice. No reasons were given but close the doors they must unless they faced a fine of $1,000 a day and possible jail time. We were all confused and when they left, the pastor said this church will remain open every Sunday for the worshippers of God. The next Sunday we got together at church and the FBI showed up and forcibly dragged our pastor away in a black suv. They told us to leave or we with our children would go to jail. The men got together with their families and they agreed to send their families home but the men of the church would stay. The FBI dragged all the men into waiting suv's and took them away. The families had no idea where the pastor or their husbands were taken to, no info was given to anyone, no matter who they asked.

Part II

DECEPTION

What happened in these stories is unthinkable, but is it? What is going on in our world now? The world is in such chaos as has never happened before in our history. What has happened to your freedoms? Do you agree the government has the right to tell you what will go into you and your children's body without actually knowing what it will do to you? After all, this is an experimental drug for Covid that only came out in three months after the pandemic hit. Little testing was done, and results were not revealed to the public, to see if this drug was safe for all people. A drug is tested for ten years or more to see how safe it would be for people. The FDA came out and stated this was an unapproved experimental drug. What does that mean other than it has not been tested long enough? Whoa, another Red Flag here. This is what it means to the insurance industry - that if anyone dies from this 'shot' and/or suffers any injuries from this 'shot,' they will not be able to collect on their life insurance. I thought I was the only 'crazy' living on the block thinking something isn't right here, until I started talking to my neighbors and I found out they were just as 'crazy' as I was. It is only within the past year that we are getting the facts. But not easily, as the CDC said it doesn't have to release their findings. Some have died from the 'shot' and others have come down with cardiac issues and others have come down with auto immune deficiencies. Dr. Peter McCullough,MD. MPH is a cardiologist, internist, and epidemiologist. I encourage you to read his book. 'Courage to Face Covid. He is an expert in his field and he cites literature on his findings which others cannot do as they have no findings to back up what they say so they use fear mongering to the public. Why were government agencies telling you natural immunity is impossible inside of your bodies and you may die if you don't take the 'shot.' Our bodies are a well oiled machine and natural immunity is one of the things that keeps it that way. (We learned later that the shot info was not true and why they lied to us.) Why in the world would they target the unvaccinated and blame them for spreading a virus they didn't have in their system? Most importantly, why did they ban treatments here in this country while the other countries were using the treatments of Ivermectin and hydroxchloroquine? The president took those drugs and was cured but were banned immediately this news was announced. Here's an important question for you, what happened to the doctor's hippocratic oath to 'Do No Harm'? It turned out their jobs were more important than their hipaa oath. They went ahead with the fear mongering knowing the dangers of this experimental drug?? To this day they are advocating CHILDREN and BABIES be given this 'shot.' How in the world is it possible for someone asking these questions to 'Trust' their doctor with their opinions? Why weren't people told to take Vitamin D3 and C at the outset of this virus? A reporter asked Fauci if he didn't have the shot then what was he taking? His answer: I take Vitamin D. What?? Did anyone hear the Congress with the Speaker of the House saying they were exempt from taking the 'shot.' They also excused the FDA and CDC and the US post office workers along with congressional pages working for them! This is where a red flag should have gone up in your head screaming to get your attention. If this virus was so dangerous, why weren't they the **first** to take the shot? Do you think they waited to see what percent of the population (**also known as guinea pigs**) would survive an experimental drug? Do you agree this 'test run' on our country and the world was to see how easy it was to manipulate Americans and others around the world? They were shocked to see how easy it was to scare people into doing whatever they said. Does this mean people with compromised health issues should get this shot? Here's what I think: I don't believe a pandemic allows the government to force an untested experimental drug on the population; I think they should have been given the choice of treatment without fear induced tactics. When we now read that elderly patients under the care of a doctor, who treated them with other meds, were seeing 90% of patients overcoming Covid. Our hats should be off to those who treated their patients with other meds in spite of being threatened of having their licenses' removed. This should have been another red flag to us that people in this country should never be threatened with helping people stay alive. Why are we mocked and made fun of for our common sense about things when others try to stuff and choke you with the idiotic ideals they believe in? We now have the CDC finally stating the truth. People with natural immunity are better off than the people who received the 'shot.' Would you agree we have a rogue government who uses threats and demeans others who don't agree with their agenda? We must fight for our first amendment rights of free speech or we will lose all our rights under the Constitution. We can no longer stand by and say 'whatever' or 'oh well'. We are in a fight for our lives and our souls. If you think God isn't going to judge you because you refused to stand up for your rights and your morals, you are wrong. This last sentence is not my words but God's.

Galatians 5:1 – "It is for freedom that Christ has set us free. Stand firm, then, and do not let yourselves be burdened again by a yoke of slavery." (NIV Study Bible)

Do you know what is going on in your child's school? When you see or hear of young teachers telling your children that doctors made a mistake and called babies a boy or girl when they were born, what do you think? Do you think God made male, female, and 'other'?

Genesis 1:27 - " So God created 'man' in his own image, in the image of God he created him, 'male and female' he created them." (NIV Study Bible)

They tell your children that parents were lied to by their doctors what their babies sex was and their parents are still lying to them. They then begin the narrative with your kids that start with 'you can only trust the government to take care of you, NOT your parents. (I hear Hitler whispering in your child's ears) They teach children they are not a boy or a girl but a transgender. Which means a girl can be a boy and a boy can be a girl or even a unicorn, for heaven's sake. Whoops, sorry God, slip of the tongue, of course not for heaven's sake. That may come under Satan 101. The next step is the mutilation of your child. They sit down and have conversations with your child about sex and how to have safe sex to 5-7 year olds. They will teach them not to be afraid of adults who want to touch their body sexually. Without your permission they will then start giving them hormone drugs. They may change their name in the schoolroom to something more appropriate for their agenda. They will tell them not to listen to their parents and to hate who they are and hate their country. How much are you willing to tolerate? Is it okay as long as it doesn't make you feel uncomfortable? Is it because you don't want to be inconvenienced? Are you living in fear of the government? Do you choose to shut your ears to what is going on cause you don't want to face it? Over two million children were pulled from the public sewer school system. Parents are opting for home school and with all the resources, it's easier to home school. Who will you choose when the government asks you to choose, them or God? Why is it good to blame Jews and Christians for any or all trouble? Is it to take the spotlight off of you so you don't come under their microscope?

Be Strong
Be Brave
Be Fearless
Here is what the bible says:

Ezekiel 3:11 - *And go, get thee to them of the captivity, unto the children of thy people, and speak unto them, and tell them, Thus saith the Lord God; whether they will hear, or whether they will forbear.* (It is up to you to hear the truth and believe or choose not to believe. God is giving you a choice here and I hope it is the one that will give you everlasting life - KJV)

Ezekiel 3:17-18 - *Son of man, I have made thee a watchman unto the house of Israel: therefore hear the word at my mouth, and give them warning from me.*
When I say unto the wicked, Thou shalt surely die; and thou givest him not warning, nor speakest to warn the wicked from his wicked way, to save his life; the same wicked man shall die in his iniquity; but his blood will I require at thine hand.
(The Lord is commanding you to tell the truth and warn of their wicked ways, for
If you fail to do so then Blood will be required by the Lord - KJV)

Luke 19:10 - *"For the Son of man is come to seek and to save that which was lost."* (KJV)

Here are some things to think about. Normal isn't coming back, Jesus is!

What is going on in this country is going on all over the world. This kind of taking away of all our freedoms has never happened here since our country gained freedom from tyranny in 1776. Have you forgotten what our founding fathers decreed when they formed the Constitution? Our country is a <u>Republic</u>, not a Democracy.

Here are some statements that you may have forgotten in this time of trouble.

In 1789 Thomas Jefferson warned that the judiciary if given too much power might ruin our Republic..and destroy our Rights.

George Washington quotes, "government is not reason, it is not eloquence; it is force! Like fire, it is a dangerous servant and a fearful master."

"The only thing necessary for evil to triumph is for good men to do nothing." Edmund Burke 1729-1797

Inscribed on our hallowed Liberty Bell are these words, "Proclaim Liberty throughout all the Land unto all the inhabitants thereof."

Isaiah 10:1-2 - Woe to those who enact unjust statutes and to those who constantly record unjust decisions, to deprive the needy of justice, and to rob the poor of My people of their rights...(NASB)

Hosea 4:6 - My people are destroyed for lack of knowledge...(KJV)

Acts 5:29 - "We must obey God rather than men." (NIV Study Bible)

Last but not least of these is II Chron. 7:14 - "If My people which are called by My name, shall humble themselves, and pray, and seek My face, and turn from their wicked ways; then will I hear from Heaven, and will forgive their sin, and will heal their land." (KJV)

Part III

PROPAGANDA ON THE LOOSE

Dictators aren't born, they are made through their life trials and thinking. Right now I believe Satan to be at the helm of our government and a fog of wickedness covers them as they carry out his commands. Only believers can see through the fog and know it for what it is.. Deception! I heard a pastor say there are more people who believe in aliens than they do in Jesus; if this is true then we are in deeper trouble than what is being poured over here.

Our founding fathers proclaimed that this country has GOD given rights! Not the government. Why am I going over these things, you may say and wasting your time reading it, Because we have forgotten our principles and morals and you live in fear of the mob that is ingratiating themselves as a force of power; which only the government has given them. This government divides its people with the voice of racism and at the same time using racism against the people. Whenever the voice of truth is spoken it is immediately defined by the media and leftist politicians that you are racist. You have to remember that 'ALL PEOPLE MATTER." Not just one class of citizens but all of us matter and we are all connected. When we don't pass along our country's history, we are doomed to repeat it. France, Finland, Canada and the Netherlands among others are in the streets protesting and resisting this global movement for one world government. The schools are no longer an institution of learning but have become a cesspool for debauchery. Is it easier to turn a blind eye to a government telling you what to do and when to do it, telling your children what to think and not to think? Do you agree with the elitists' statements that "you will own nothing and be happy?" Are you comfortable putting believers in internment camps because they don't fit in with you? Will you be okay with judging who will stay in their house and who will go to an internment camp? What did you think when they opened our borders and let drug cartels and sex traffiking of women and children cross our borders with no stopping the numbers? We now have over 2-3 million illegals in the country and we have no idea where they are. They could be in your community waiting to strike your town or city. Why is it okay to give all these illegals social security numbers or our tax paid goods and services including infant formula stored in a warehouse while our own citizens had no access to baby formula or other necessities? Why was there no outrage against this?

Acts 17:26 declares - First, God himself established the very idea of nations and borders. "From one man he (God) made all the nations, that they should inhabit the whole earth; and he marked out their appointed times in history and the boundaries of their lands." (NIV)

Will you be okay with the government telling you who will go to prison and who will not? How about a Congress who supports and incites violence in people because they can't get their own way? Why is it that liberals want to sue republicans for supposed crimes that they themselves are guilty of? Do you think it strange that they are so quick to call everyone else a racist, but when illegals show up in their city, they cry from the treetops how unchristian and trafficking of border people arriving in their city is? They quickly accuse border states of racism, states who are so overloaded with illegals that the citizens can no longer leave their house without being in fear of their lives. They actually called in the national guard and the military to have illegals removed from their community, but they are Not willing to do the same for the border states. Isn't this an act of racism on their part? After all, diversity is the constant we keep hearing from them. Actions speak louder than words and I hope all of you can see this and know it for what it is-lies and deception. Diversity and racism is for the rest of us but not for them. We too had small towns where we could ride our bikes and browse through our town without being assaulted or be fearful of who we may meet on the street. They took that from us by flying these illegals and cartels to our small towns, but God forbid it should happen in their backyards of Martha Vineyard, New York, San Francisco, Chicago and others who are sanctuary cities. I can hear your brain running a mile a minute from here. This person is crazy, she's off her rocker, I'm not reading anymore of this fake rhetoric. Hold on before you chuck the book, I listened to your confused brain but here is a question for you, **what if I'm right**? **What then**?

    Once again, because we are so inundated on an hourly and daily basis so that our focus skills are below normal, do you agree and are you okay with the government taking over the job of raising your children? When you have no choice but to put your child in government child care and government run schools by Marxist, Communists, or Socialists, how is that going to sit with you? How important is it to you that your children have a better life than you did growing up? Do you think a socialist government will do a better job of raising your children?

    What is your opinion of 'drag queens', in their attire, reading story books to your children in a public library or maybe in your school library and explaining how it's okay for adults to hug and touch your children? What about schools having a 'letter' for children to change their sex without parents knowledge? Did you know that a pedophil is labeled as having a disease by the current culture in this country? Nothing is off their list of the most extreme teachings of evil. Most parents would think this is dangerous learning for 5-7 year olds. Other parents think this is okay for their kids to understand different people in the world and will allow their children to be exposed to such demon culture. Especially when the drag queen ends up being arrested for child pornography and indecent exposure. If we follow the justice system in today's culture, I'm not sure this person was given a slap on the wrist and sent back on the streets with a feather in their cap. The liberals are very big with reality shows. Unfortunately their platforms include the fake media which reaches a lot of people and these people still believe what they hear and what they see. I believe they 'stage' events to twist the minds of people who see it and actually believe it is real, not knowing the reality behind the scenes. I can't say it enough, We Live in Dangerous Times.

'The book of the bible relates how people in the end times will be blindfolded to the truth and they will turn away from it.'

Will you allow deception to blindfold you to the truth? Will you just believe everything and not investigate on your own what is truth and what is false? Will you be okay with the government shutting down churches? What will you think when they say worship is against their law? What will you think when you are called a religious extremist? Will it be okay to imprison anyone who says the word 'Jesus?' When churches are afraid to stand up to the evil in this world, they not only do an injustice to their congregation but to God himself. I don't know where you stand in your faith as you read this but I can tell you now that the younger people in this country are turning back to the law and to the church and their faith in God. You can see it in the ProLife movement. When Roe vs Wade was overturned, there were churches who did not think it appropriate to celebrate as they didn't want to hurt anyone's feelings. I am sure God and his angels were celebrating while your voice was silent. That was a day of celebration that should have been heard around the world. Why is the church's voice silent and not standing up to what is going wrong in this country? Why are they not teaching their congregation to speak out against the tyranny in this country? If the church stands in fear then they will have a congregation that is fearful also. Now that same fight for human life in the womb is taken up by each of the states where it was supposed to be from the beginning. There is no scripture that says God is okay with abortion. No matter how hard you look. Where does your church stand? Where do you stand?

Remember God's words:

Matthew 18:6 - "But whoever causes one of these little ones who believe in Me to sin, it would be better for him if a millstone were hung around his neck, and he were drowned in the depth of the sea." (NKJV)

There may come a day when everyone in the world will see a hologram or a similar event in the clouds on their TV or a phone or a computer. It could be something else altogether but one thing is for sure, it will be a WorldWide event. There are many who have lost their moral compass in this world and will believe whatever is told to them. This image may say that they are Jesus or God and you must worship him. If you don't know Jesus and his teachings and who he is, you are going to be deceived into thinking an image is actually Christ. The AntiChrist will be able to do many signs and wonders also, he is afterall, 'The Great Deceiver.' Remember this, AntiChrist will try to duplicate everything the Son of God did. This is one of the ways he will deceive you. He will be using technology that we have allowed to ingratiate into our lives. AI and chips implanted into our bodies are on our horizon, and our cell phones will be used against us. He will know where and what we are doing and maybe even thinking. It is not beyond the realm of possibilities. I suggest here that the Seed of the AntiChrist is already here on earth and is the reason the whole world is in turmoil. I suggest that if you are in the 'feel good' church, you may want to look around for a church who is ahead of the game and preaching about the times we are in and how God is moving among us and His Truth shall be upheld no matter the consequences. Find or start a bible study group and get to know what the Lord says in these days of fear and uncertainty. If you don't find a bible group near you then pray and talk to god on your own. Let him know of the love you feel for him inside your heart. Fear mongering has become a fine art of deception for a government who is afraid of its people. It is the way to control the people and feed their greed for power. God makes a way when there is no way!

It is my opinion that a great event will occur before the midterm elections and our election process will once again be overturned. Right now Congress is passing a law to change the way we count the ballots, with the VP having the last word on your vote. Mail-in ballots will only be admitted, they say. Remember our history and know that dictators do <u>Not go Quietly</u> into the sunset hanging their heads. They are capable of doing anything and everything to keep themselves in power. If we as FREE people do not guard ourselves and demand to right any wrongs, then we as a FREE country will bow to the tyranny of the elite and will become under the rule of Marxism!!

John 14:6 - Jesus answered, I am the way and the truth and the life. No one comes to the Father except through me. (NIV Study Bible)

How far will you go to protect your freedoms, protect your family, and or protect your home or stand up for your friends when trouble comes knocking on their door or yours?? What about standing up for God? **God is watching.** The devil isn't the only one in a harvest for souls, God is also in a harvest, for your spirit and soul.

2 Timothy 3: 2-5 - But mark this: There will be terrible times in the last days. People will be lovers of themselves, lovers of money, boastful, proud, abusive, disobedient to their parents, ungrateful, unholy, without love, unforgiving, slanderous, without self-control, brutal, not lovers of the good, treacherous, rash, conceited, lovers of pleasure rather than lovers of God - having a form of godliness but denying its power. Have nothing to do with them. (NIV Study Bible)

Part IV

REMEMBER THESE THINGS:

They have pushed many of you to the edge and you are now learning how to push back. This regime knows it cannot win people who have known freedom most of their lives. Are we so far gone that we have forgotten the evil leaders of countries in our past and the atrocities they perpetrated on their people? This is Hitler's playbook as he took over Germany. First thing he did was lie to the people and say he will give them freedom and they will flourish in Germany. The next thing he did was to turn people against one another, in this instance, to hate the Jews. *(In this country the government is using racism)*. He got rid of the church when he threw the pastors into prison. He caused distrust of the police and caused Jew's to hide in fear of being thrown into the ovens. Overburdened people with unfair taxes. Controlled all the balloting and he controlled the media. In our instance the government opened the borders and overburdened the economy and the people with unfair taxes. Sound familiar? He knew he still could not win over all the people so his next move was to take control of the children. As young as ten, twelve, and fourteen years old were put into the military and mind control was used to hate their parents and the Jews and to Love the government. These children would turn in their parents and their neighbors to the

Nazi's. So what is the big picture here? The answer is in **your** children. ***If you Control the Children then you Control the Future!*** Is the truth starting to penetrate yet? Why do the schools say parents should have no input over what is taught in the schools? Parents, up to 2020, had a lot of input in their children's school studies. We pay the teachers salaries to teach our children education in math, english, history, reading etc. We now have the school having the authority to sit with your child and ask them to change who they are into another sex or even an animal? Sounds unbelievable? Some schools have litter boxes in their rooms for children who associate with being an animal. What you say! I don't believe it. Really? Nothing is beyond their means. This is learned behavior, I believe, that comes from the school. They can change your children in the way they think, the way they behave, and the way they believe. Remember - They can even give them hormones to alter who they are **Without Your Permission!** They can give your children abortions without your permission.

If there's ever a time to stand up for your children and protect them, <u>Today</u> is that time. Run for your school board and replace the persons who are implementing these destructive agenda's. Go to your schools and talk with your teachers, your principal, and others who have communication with your child. Ask to see the curriculum and the books for your children. Ask to see the library of your children's books. If the school puts you off or stops you from wanting to do any of these things - RUN as fast as you can away from this type of school. They work for you, not the other way around. Recent polls show over 2 million children have been taken out of the public sewer school system. Home schooling children is going way up, to the point of some politicians wanting to dismantle the public school system. Until something is done soon, you must push back as if you have everything to lose, **Because You Do.**

Mark 9:36-37 - He took a little child and had him stand among them. Taking him in his arms, he said to them, Whoever welcomes one of these little children in my name welcomes me: and whoever welcomes me does not welcome me but the one who sent me. (NIV Study Bible)

*Mark 3:24-25 - And if a kingdom be divided against itself, that kingdom cannot stand. And if a house be divided against itself, that house cannot stand. (NIV Bible Study)
*Mark 3: 29-30 - But he that shall blaspheme against the Holy Ghost hath never forgiveness, but is in danger of eternal damnation: Because they said, He hath an unclean spirit. KJV

Shaiki Horowitz, an Israeli former general, said this when asked why there are no school shootings. He said in Israel this is how they protect their children:
They have a fence around their schools
Their gates have armed guards
They have frequent drills in case they are attacked, they will know what to do.
    (In 2022, Israel had the most visitors to their country than it ever has in its history.)

    Did you know that the archeological discoveries in this world and especially the Middle East and Israel are finding writings and etchings on the walls that verify the bible and its contents? The same names in the bible are being found on scrolls and the pictures on walls. The Walls of Jericho and remains of the Temple Mount that was destroyed twice have been uncovered. The city of David has been uncovered as well as other kings. The bible is not a storybook of fictitious names and places. It is the Truth of the Word. The mysteries of the bible are finally coming to life right before our eyes.

Do you notice the only people who have fences and gates and armed guards are the people in power? Why are our children not granted that safety also in our schools?

These people in power plan in years what they want to happen in your country, yes, You're country! We were all asleep at the wheel living our lives and believing the government was looking out for us and we had their protection, until this happened. They know they need to do something soon or they will lose everything they have been working toward. They are sore losers and will do anything and everything to make sure they don't lose their power in this country. They know if they lose, they will be brought up on charges for crimes against the constitution and crimes against humanity.

They are flooding our country with illegals and drug cartels to help them in their quest for power. These millions of illegals in our country are being taken care of with our tax dollars. We are helping them to spread these people in the middle of the night all over the country by keeping silent. Tell your governor these people need to go to the steps of government, to the houses of Congress and be dropped off by bus. SPEAK UP AND SAY IT IS WRONG!! Contact your representatives today. Don't give them a free pass if they don't or won't answer you. You keep going until you get an answer and then you hold them to it. The illegals will be able to vote for them which will cancel your vote for freedom. Venezuela is emptying their prisons of violent criminals and sending them to American borders. Don't you see what is going on here people? Drugs are entering our country in amounts that were unheard of before. Eventually these drugs including fentanyl, which they also have made in pill form and come wrapped in pretty colored papers for small hands to unwrap easily, will get into the hands of your children or loved ones, either knowingly or unknowingly. We are in a war today. Not with weapons and physical fighting on the ground but a spiritual war for your soul. Stand up to the evil you see perpetrated everyday in our country. Stand up for those who are making a difference in our government.

There is a line being drawn. You will soon have to ask yourself, am I on this side, or am I on the other side. Each side represents either evil or good. The choice is yours. Making a good choice is not going to be easy. Evil doesn't like to be thwarted and there will be consequences to pay. You will need all the strength inside of you, all the prayer you can pray every day for you and your family to get through this. You will not be able to close your eyes anymore to the evil going on around you.

The murders in this country have risen to heights that have been unheard of in our past. Why? The protestors are destroying businesses, burning down business, and harming people to the point some have died from their injuries. People walking into businesses grabbing cash and other things and walking back out. The police are now told to not arrest misdemeanors so it is no wonder the business owner has to protect himself and his business against the wrongdoings of others! No one is arrested and no one is accountable. When the person protecting others or their business with a firearm they become victimized by the Congress and the media. It's not an easy job fighting for truth. They created the distrust of police and in that repeated rhetoric were able to defund the police so they could no longer do their job. When these protestors were arrested, they were bailed out by persons in government. They threaten people with their hate speech, they threaten Supreme Court members without accountability. Our own Senate, except for a few members vehemently speaking out against this, is silent on this. We have the power of the vote to put who we want in charge. If we have members who are lukewarm and can't stand up for the citizens in this country, then we certainly don't want them to keep sitting in a senate seat with their mouths wired shut unwilling to fight for this country and our freedom and getting Paid for it. Bring back term limits for all, not just the president.

There are two tiers of justice in this country; one for government and one for the citizens who are against the government. I can't make this any plainer than what I have written here. Do the research on who is running for government in your state. Yes, it will take time to do this but our Freedoms are at stake. Call your Republicans or Democrats and ask for a dossier on all the candidates running in your state. Words Matter. We are all Watchmen.

There will be many things happening in the world as the practice of sin and deception leads to more deception. The war will be for our children. <u>Don't forget it.</u> Many people don't believe we are in the End of Days but I for one believe it. No other time in history has our world been in such turmoil. There is no place you can go, for what is happening here is happening all over the world. The turning away of people to the truth, the threat of major war, the global reset of the world, the onset of a one world government. The news media is setting us up for the appearance of world famine. Another pandemic to lock us down or the slaughter of cattle and to stop farming except to grow plant based food for all the people except the elitists who will still have their steak and eggs, etc. Sounds impossible? Everything that has happened to us sounds impossible and yet here we are today in the middle of it. Wake up because we are running out of time and resources. The government is giving our food supply reserves and our fuel reserves away to Europe and China. Israel is being threatened by Russia but not for the reason you think, I believe it will be because of its oil and strategic location. It will be Iran who forces their hand. America keeps moving on the wrong track as it negotiates a nuclear deal against Israel's warnings. The bible says, if we turn our backs on Israel, then woe will be unto us and others who turn their backs on them. Right now Iran is threatening Israel with a missile strike. You say what's this got to do with me? Plenty! If these threats turn into a pending war which I think it will, according to Israel, then this will herald in the 'Prince of Peace." He may very well turn into being the AntiChrist. Everyone will be in awe of him. He will have much charisma.

Joel 2:28 - And it shall come to pass afterward, that I will pour out my spirit upon all flesh; and your sons and your daughters shall prophesy, your old men shall dream dreams, your young men shall see visions: (KJV)

*2Peter 1:19 - 21 We also have the word of the prophets as confirmed beyond doubt. And you will do well to pay attention to it, as to a lamp shining in a dark place, until the day dawns and the morning star rises in your hearts. (KJV)

Haggai 2:7 - And I will shake all nations, and the desire of all nations shall come: and I will fill this house with glory, saith the LORD of hosts. (KJBible)

Jude 11:17-19 - But, dear friends, remember what the apostles of our Lord Jesus Christ foretold. They said to you, "In the last times" there will be scoffers who will follow their own ungodly desires." These are the men who divide you, who follow mere natural instincts and do not have the Spirit." (NIV Study Bible)

The Lord says to occupy until he returns.

Here are some signs of end times to watch for.

Red Heifer
Pre Tribulation wars
Two raptures(one with the church rapture and the dead rise and then believers will be raptured) the last rapture will be for the final martyrs and those who chose to believe in Jesus in the end)
No buying or selling without a chip in your right hand or forehead.
Temple will be built in the middle of tribulation.
AntiChrist stops sacrifices. (Part of deception)
Two witnesses protect temple builders.
Entire world will be watching.
Feast of trumpets

The Lord uses the Moon, the Sun, and the stars as signs and wonders and on the earth dismay among nations.

There are questions in this book you will eventually have to answer. Maybe not today, but I believe soon. Have Faith in God.

By Lynda Like

1 Timothy 5 verse 8 - If anyone does not provide for his relatives, and especially for his immediate family, he has denied the faith and is worse than an unbeliever. (NIV Study Bible)

List of front line doctors who have books out to help you maneuver around a pandemic. How much is too much for your body to handle numerous vaccines, tested and untested.

Dr. Avery Jackson, Neurosurgeon
The God Prescription

Dr. Peter McCullough, MD MPH
The Courage to Face Covid-19

Dr. Jeff Barke, MD
Covid 19 A Physicians Take on the Exaggerated Fear of Coronavirus

Dr. Richard Urso - Globalsummit.org

The Journal of Immunology

References for homeschooling children:

Contact your state representative for materials
Here is a partial list in Pa. - I see you must file an affidavit each year to homeschool:
https://www.education.pa.gov › K-12 › Home Education and Private Tutoring
Queen Homeschool Supplies
Lamp Post Home School
Christian Homeschool Assoc.
BridgeWay Academy
The Homeschool Awakening - AAAA
Celebratekids - AAAA
K-12.com
Also Coalition of Homeschoolers - in your county and area + there are resources.

Check out homeschoolers help and support groups in your area. Moms and kids get together and help one another.
    Look for homeschool in your state and verify the materials are what you want your child to learn.
    There are many avenues for homeschoolers now and for kids to enjoy social events.
    There are teachers out there who opted out of the school system and offer their tutoring services.
    Your child is worth every effort and investment to keep them safe and educated to your standards and not the world.

You can take any one of the prayers listed in the Bible under Psalms in this book. This is the one I start with. Matthew 6:9-13 (NIV)

Our Father in heaven, hallowed be your name, your kingdom come, your will be done, on earth as it is in Heaven. Give us today our daily bread. Forgive us our debts as we also have forgiven our debtors. And lead us not into temptation, but deliver us from the evil one.
Or
My Father in Heaven, I pray for the repentance of my sins. I ask you to come into my heart.. You can continue with Ephesians prayer.

Ephesians 2:4-5 (NIV)
    Another bible verse:
O Lord, because of Your love and compassion over me, save me by Your grace so that I will be worthy of your blessings, in the name of Jesus.
                  AMEN

**Congratulations -
You are now part of the Army of God.
Stay in Prayer**

CPSIA information can be obtained
at www.ICGtesting.com
Printed in the USA
BVHW030506191222
654519BV00017B/664